Ten Terrible Dinosaurs

Paul Stickland

Ragged Bears

10 Ten terrible dinosaurs

standing in a line,

soon began to mess about,

until there were...

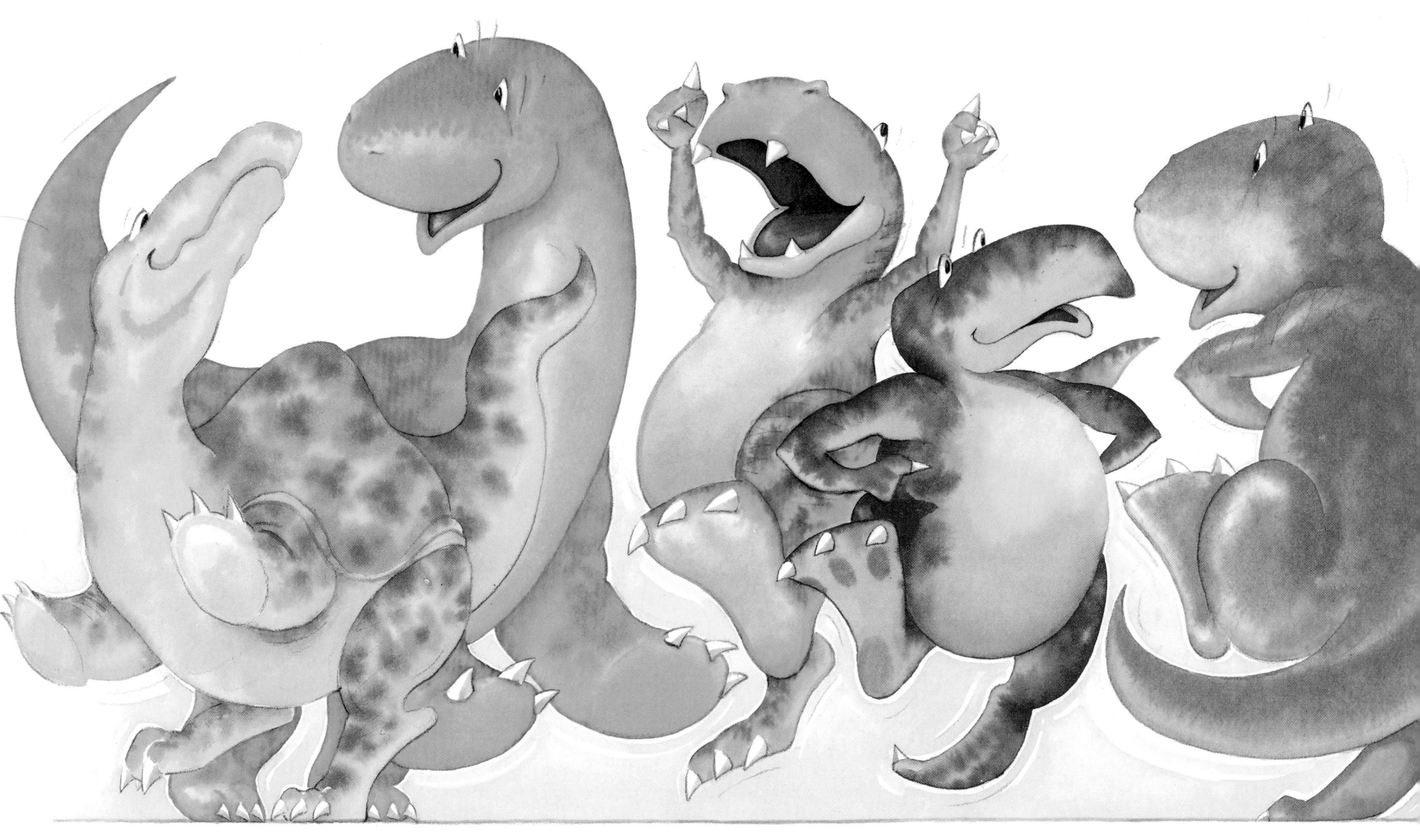

9 Nine enormous dinosaurs,

their dancing was just great,

but one was much too spiky,

so soon there were...

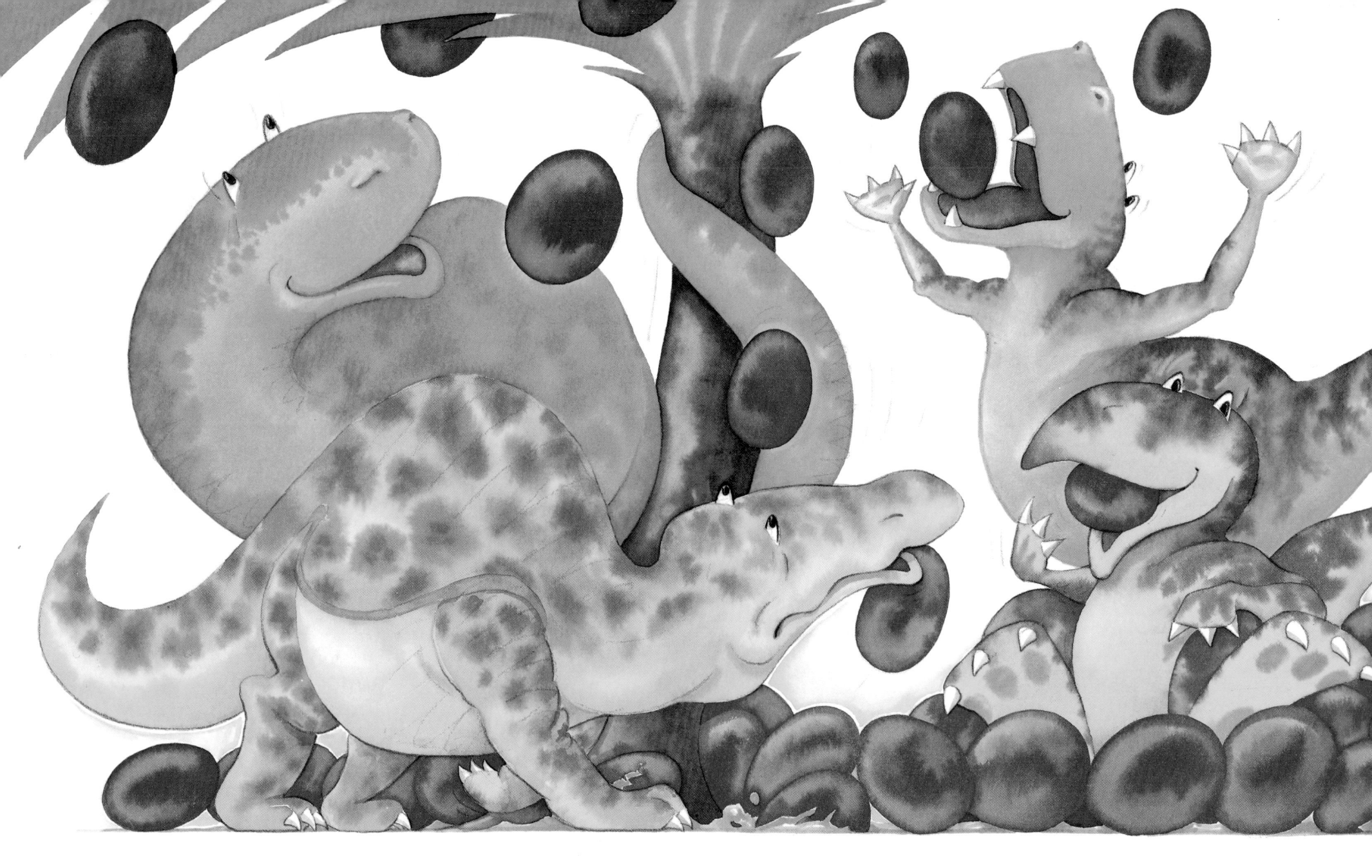

8 Eight elated dinosaurs

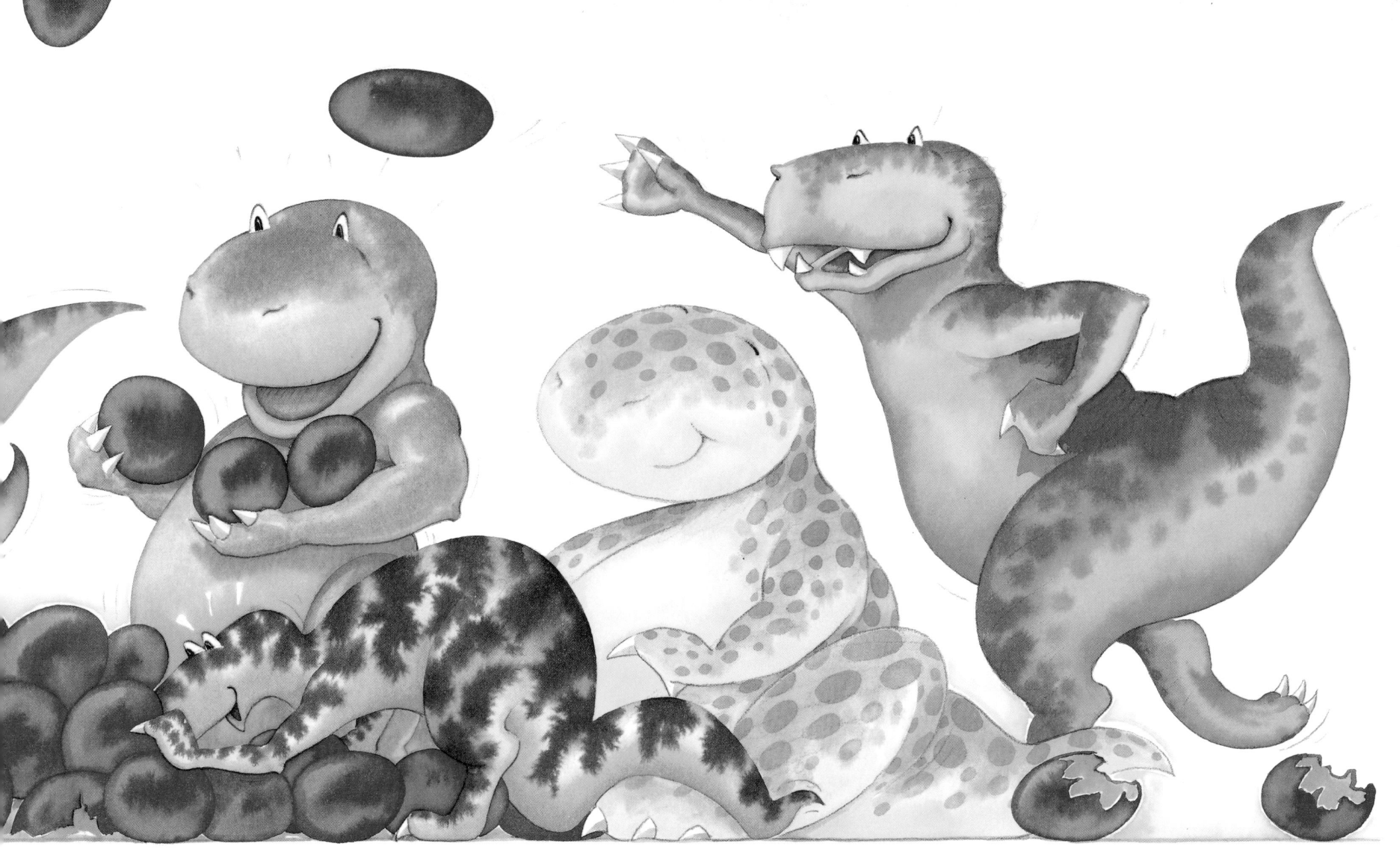

thought they were in heaven,

but one nearly popped,

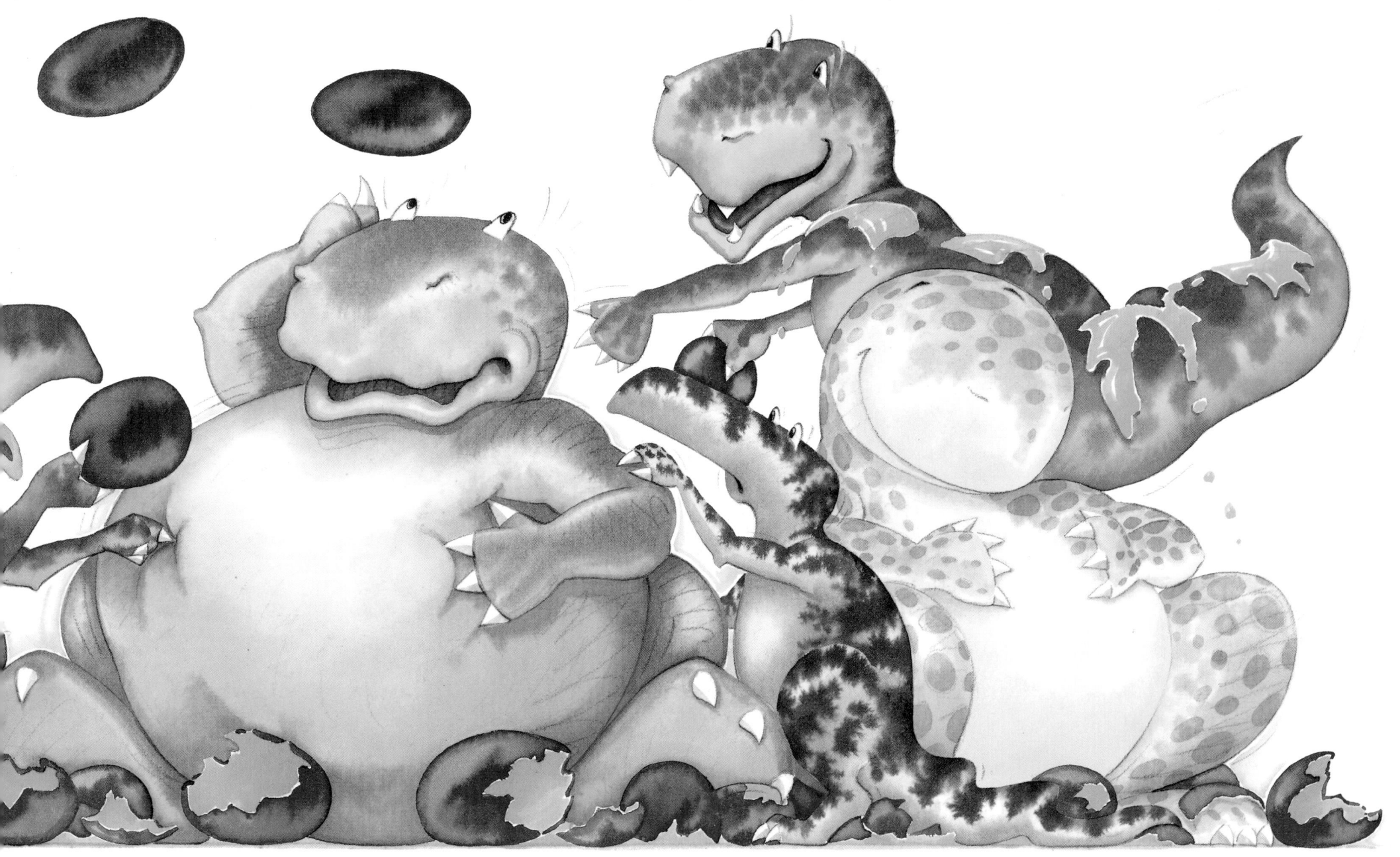

so then there were...

7 Seven silly dinosaurs

playing silly tricks

one went wrong,

so then there were...

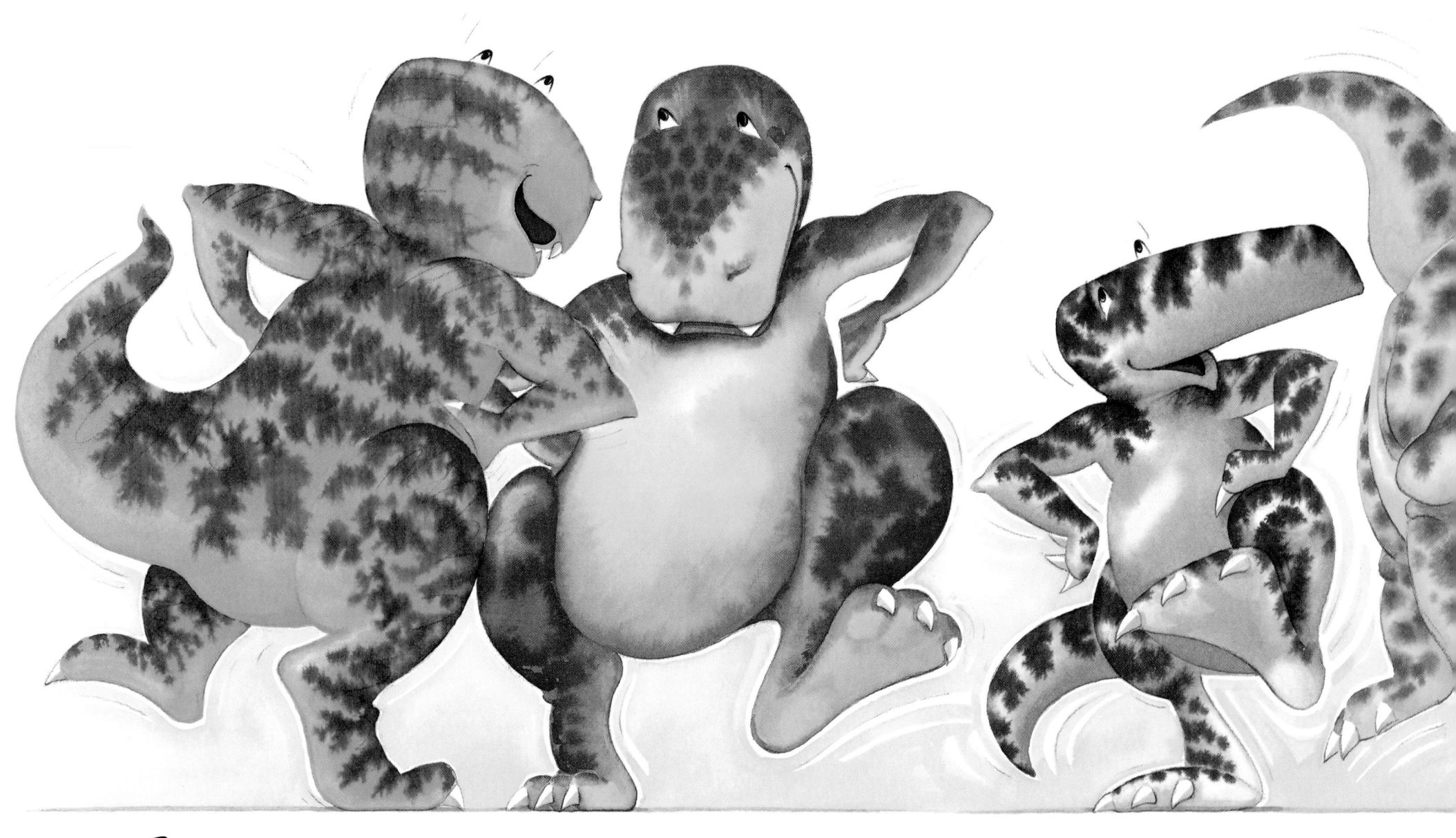

6 Six stamping dinosaurs

did a crazy jive,

one got tangled up,

so then there were...

5 Five feisty dinosaurs,

fierce in tooth and claw,

one's mum said "STOP THAT!"

so then there were...

4 Four fearless dinosaurs

hiding in a tree,

one got stuck,

so then there were...

3 Three eager dinosaurs

tried and almost flew,

one really did,

so then there were...

2 Two tetchy dinosaurs,

far too tired to run,

one got taken home,

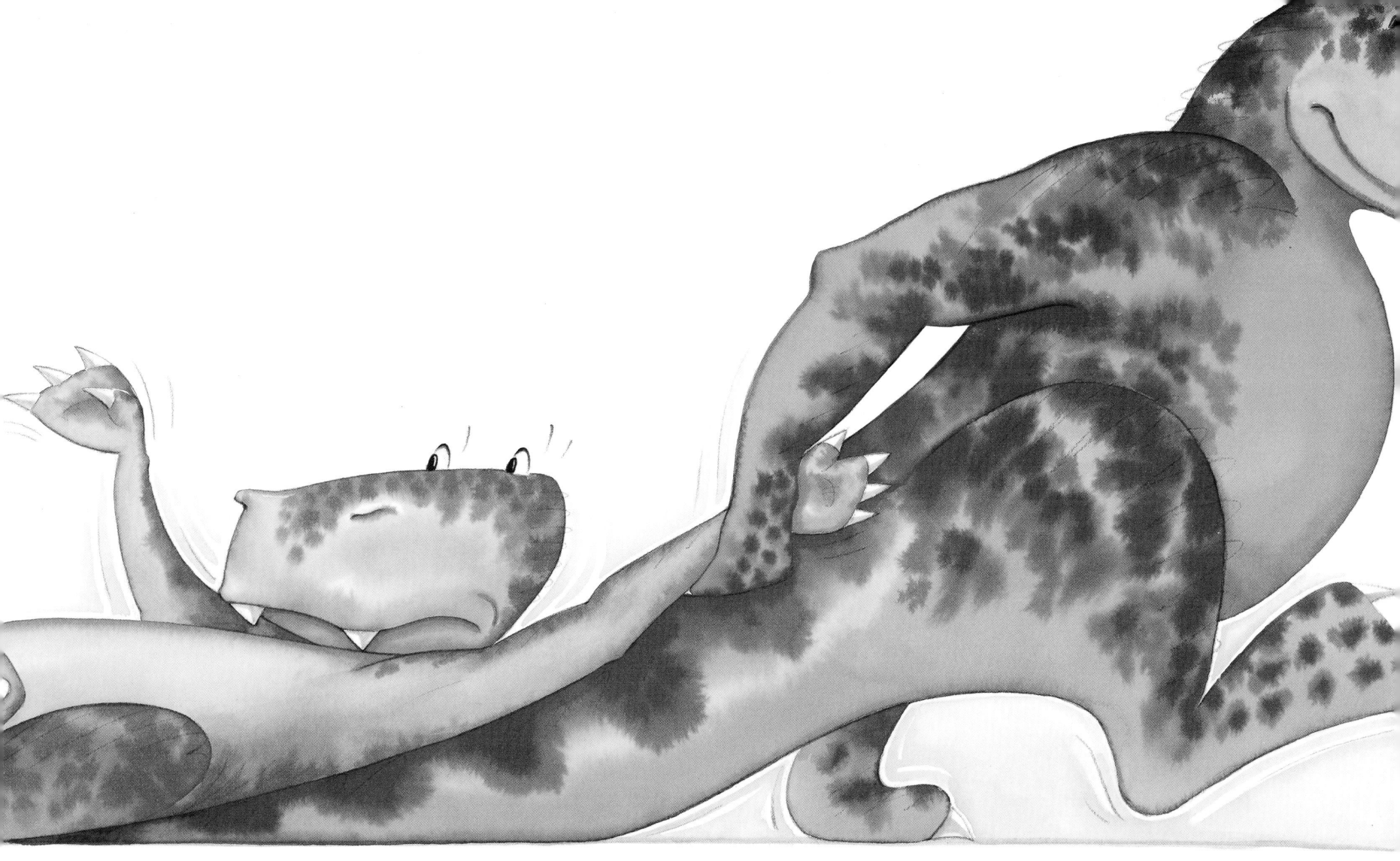

so then there was...

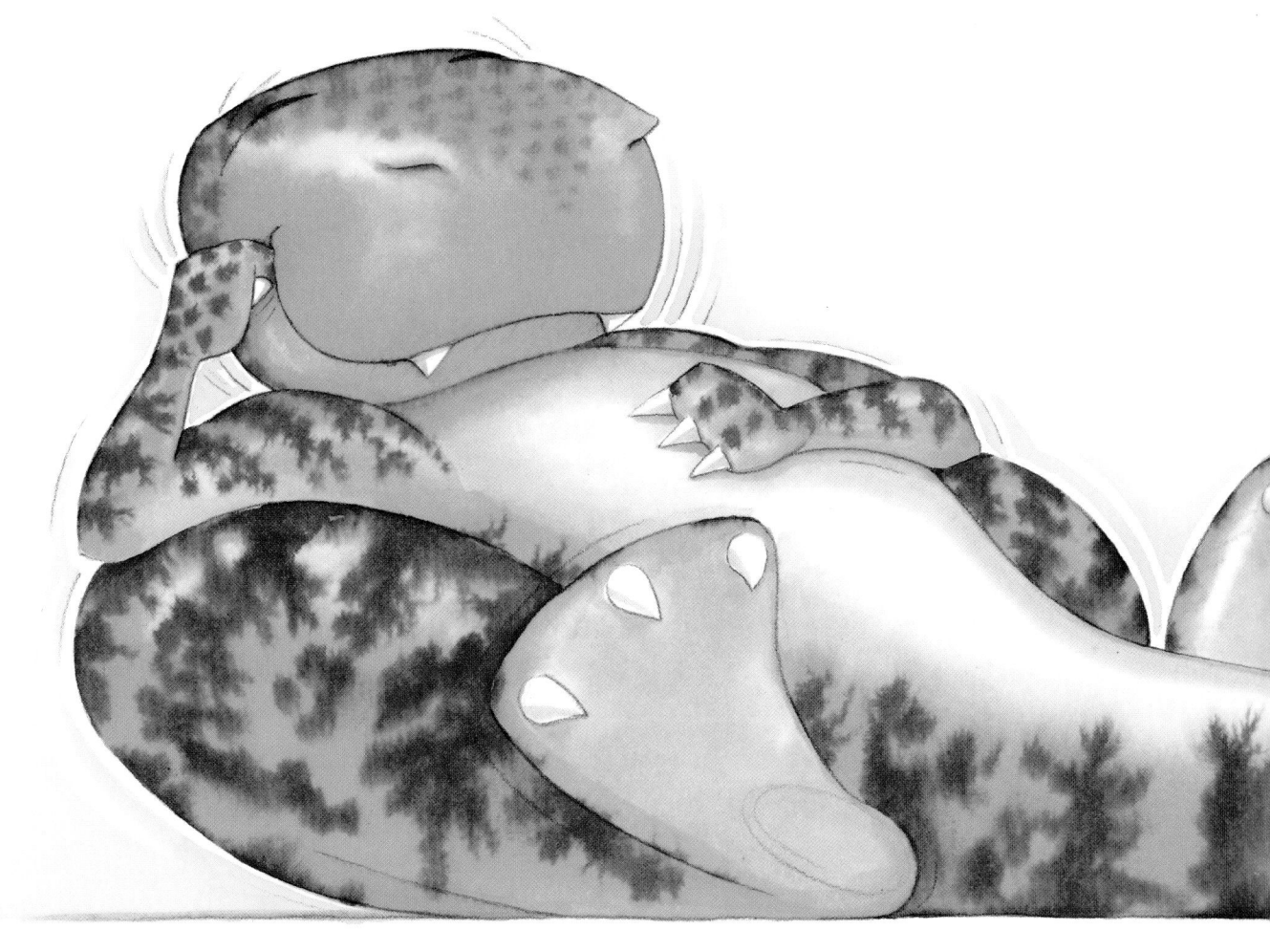

1 One weary dinosaur

soon began to snore,

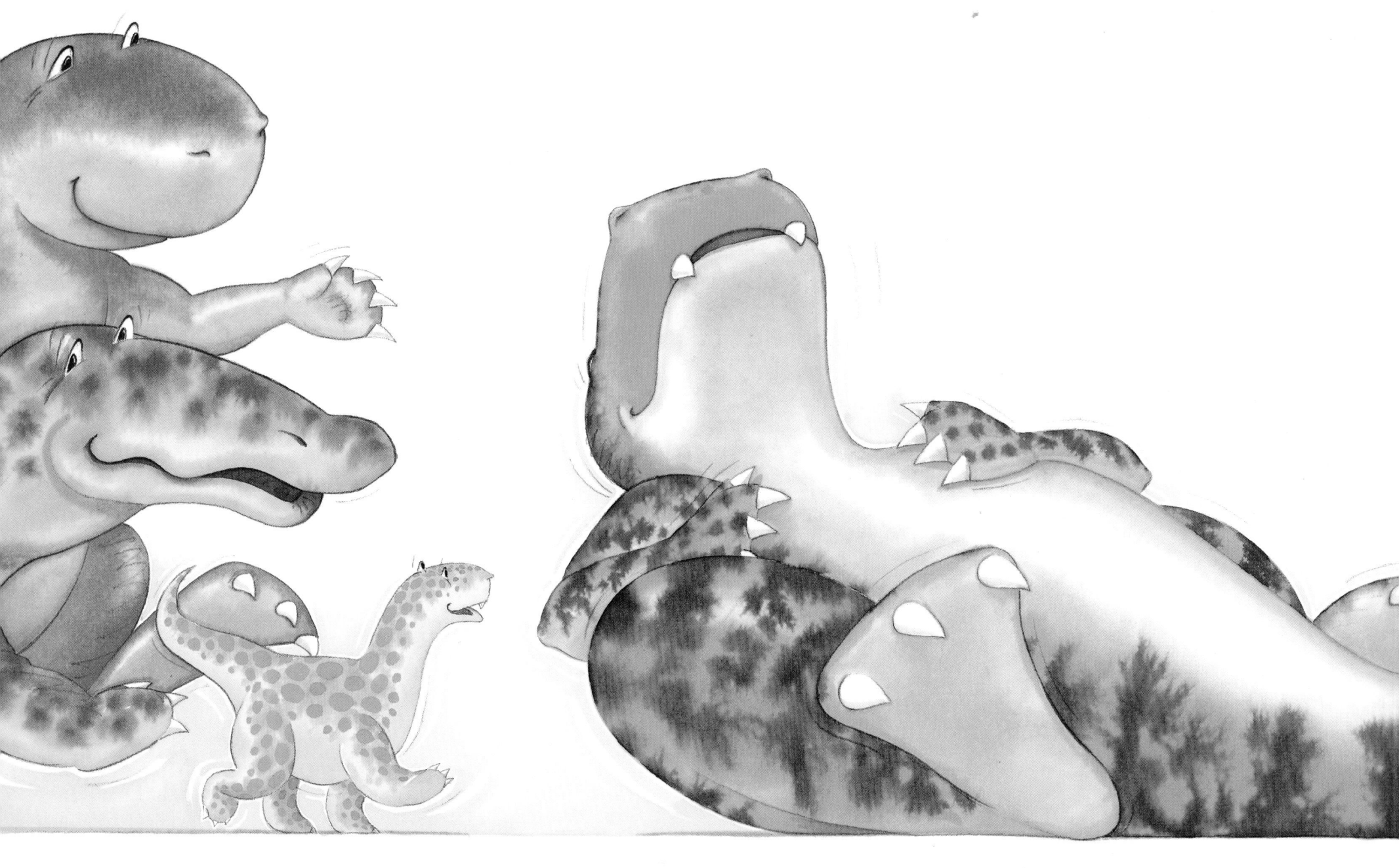

his friends crept up on him

and suddenly yelled...

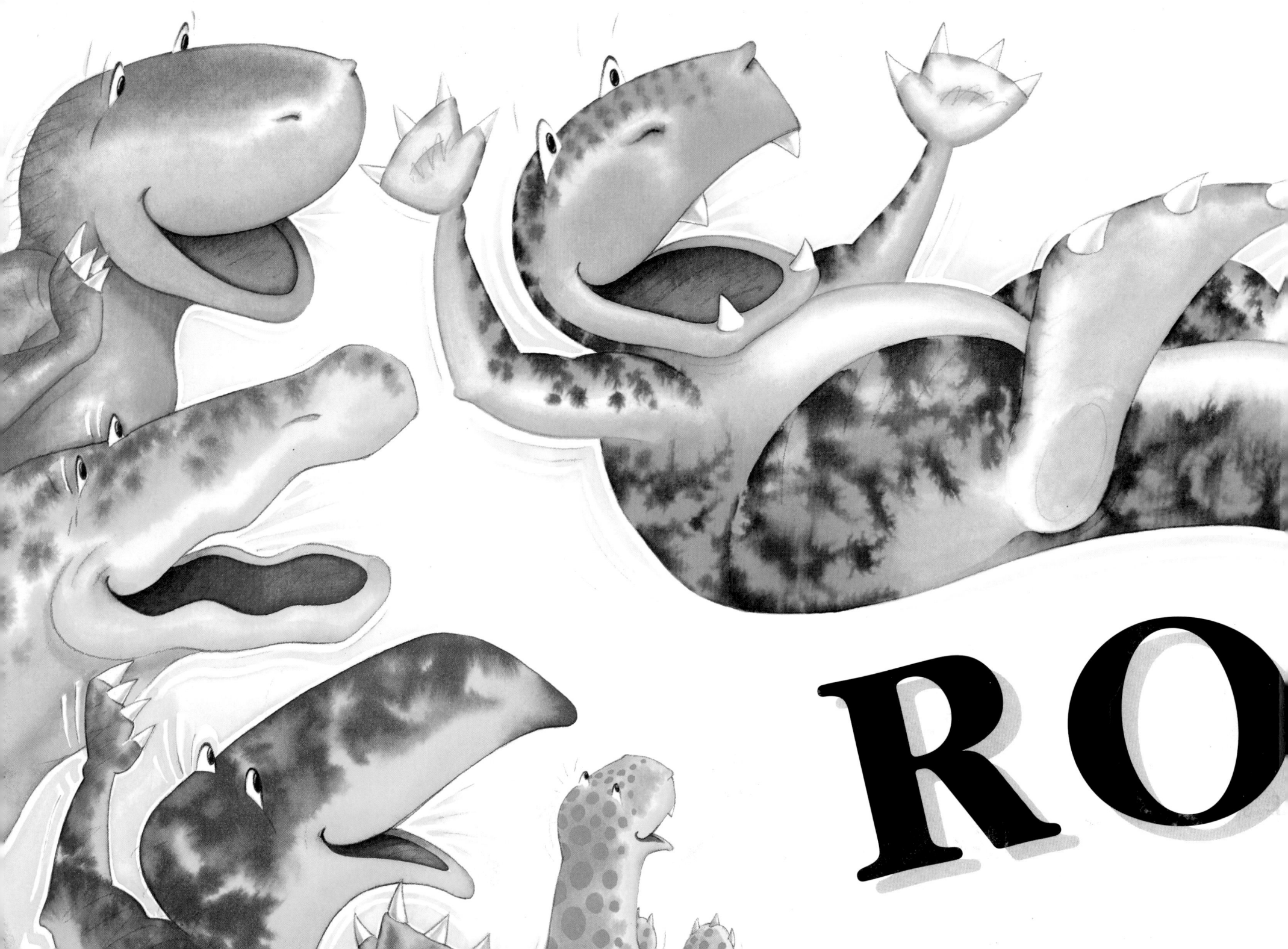

RO

Other books by Paul Stickland for dinosaur fans:

DINOSAUR ROAR!
"Children are captivated from beginning to end"
Child Education

SWAMP STOMP (POP-UP)
"Paul Stickland's dinosaurs have a freshness that make them stand out in every sense." The Bookseller

First published in Great Britain in 1997
by Ragged Bears Limited,
Ragged Appleshaw, Andover,
Hampshire SP11 9HX
Reprinted in 1999
Text and illustration copyright © 1997 by Paul Stickland

A CIP record of this book is available from the British Library

ISBN 1 85714 136 9

Printed in Singapore